DRAGON ON THE LOOSE

MARTY CHAN

ILLUSTRATED BY GRACE CHEN

ORCA BOOK PUBLISHERS

Text copyright © Marty Chan 2024
Illustrations copyright © Grace Chen 2024

Published in Canada and the United States in 2024 by Orca Book Publishers.
orcabook.com

All rights are reserved, including those for text and data mining, AI training and similar technologies. No part of this publication may be reproduced or transmitted in any form or by any means, electronic or mechanical, including photocopying, recording or by any information storage and retrieval system now known or to be invented, without permission in writing from the publisher.

Library and Archives Canada Cataloguing in Publication
Title: Dragon on the loose / Marty Chan ; illustrated by Grace Chen.
Names: Chan, Marty, author. | Chen, Grace (Illustrator), illustrator.
Series: Orca echoes.
Description: Series statement: Orca echoes
Identifiers: Canadiana (print) 20230482910 | Canadiana (ebook) 20230482929 | ISBN 9781459834217 (softcover) | ISBN 9781459834224 (PDF) | ISBN 9781459834231 (EPUB)
Subjects: LCGFT: Novels.
Classification: LCC PS8555.H39244 D73 2024 | DDC jC813/.54—dc23

Library of Congress Control Number: 2023941061

Summary: In this partially illustrated early chapter book, two young friends bring a friendly dragon statue to life and must find a way to help her get home.

Orca Book Publishers is committed to reducing the consumption of nonrenewable resources in the production of our books. We make every effort to use materials that support a sustainable future.

Orca Book Publishers gratefully acknowledges the support for its publishing programs provided by the following agencies: the Government of Canada, the Canada Council for the Arts and the Province of British Columbia through the BC Arts Council and the Book Publishing Tax Credit.

Cover and interior artwork by Grace Chen
Design by Dahlia Yuen
Edited by Debbie Rogosin

Printed and bound in Canada.

27 26 25 24 • 1 2 3 4

CHAPTER ONE

"Kyle, take your hand out of the lion's mouth!" I yelled.

With his hand inside the stone lion's mouth, my best friend scrunched up his face and asked, "Why, Hailey?"

"Because you're doing it the wrong way," I said.

"No, this seems right," Kyle said. Ever since I'd met him in third grade, he's always wanted to do things his way. He hasn't changed in three years.

"You won't get any good luck that way," I said.

"How do you know, Hailey?"

"My grandpa taught me," I said.

Grandpa Wong and I used to visit the China Gate lions once a month. First we'd go to the dim sum restaurant around the corner, where I'd order my favorite dish—shrimp dumplings. He always ordered something different.

One time it was chicken feet. I'd stared at the slimy claws on the plate and pushed away from the table.

"Ew," I said. "No way. I'm not eating feet. Gross."

He laughed as he plucked one of the feet off the plate with his chopsticks and placed it in front of me.

"You'll like it. Tastes like chicken," he joked.

I shook my head, crossed my arms and clamped my lips shut.

"Hailey, don't be afraid of a new thing. It might be the start of your next adventure."

"It looks weird," I said.

"The sooner you try it, the quicker we can get to the China Gate and make a wish."

"Can I make my wish now? Because I wish you didn't order chicken feet," I said.

He laughed again. "Try it, Hailey. Trust me."

I picked up the foot with my fingers and bit into the flesh. It tasted like chicken skin with a salty sauce. "It's not that bad." I took another bite.

"See?" he said with a smile, taking a foot for himself.

I'd finished the rest of mine.

After lunch, Grandpa Wong and I would walk to the China Gate, where a golden roof supported by red pillars formed an arch over the street. Chinese lion statues sat on either side of the gate. Mounted on top, two Chinese dragon statues that looked like rolling ocean waves met in the center. The wingless creatures seemed to watch over the street like guardians.

Grandpa Wong would lift me onto one of the lions' pedestals. He said if I rubbed the stone ball in its mouth, the lion might grant me a wish. I always wished for the same thing—another dim sum with my favorite grandpa.

The last time I made my wish, it didn't come true. Grandpa Wong died a week later. The next day a windstorm blew one of the dragons off the arch and destroyed it. I felt like the remaining dragon—alone.

"Why did we come here today, Hailey?" Kyle asked.

"Tomorrow the city is tearing the gate down so they can dig a tunnel for the subway."

"What are they going to do with it?" Kyle adjusted the chin strap of his bicycle helmet.

"My dad told me the gate's going into storage."

"That's too bad. How am I going to get my wish?"

I grinned. "You always want the same thing." I fished a baggie full of Chewy Worms out of my backpack. He licked his lips at the sight of the candy.

"My wish came true!"

"You're so predictable." I tossed the baggie at him.

He plucked out a worm while I climbed onto the lion's pedestal. I rubbed the stone ball the way Grandpa Wong had taught me, rolling my hand over it from left to right. I looked up. The remaining dragon had been Grandpa Wong's favorite part of the China Gate. Mine too. I'd always thought the dragon and Grandpa Wong would be here forever.

"I wish I could save you," I whispered.

The ball began to tingle under my hand. I yanked it out of the lion's mouth.

"What was that?" I muttered.

"What's wrong, Hailey?" Kyle asked. "Make the wrong wish?"

"It's nothing," I said, rubbing my palm. I slowly reached into the lion's mouth again and touched the ball. It vibrated against my palm. A jolt of electricity stung my hand as a crack of thunder echoed in my ears. Was it from the sky or the lion's mouth? I couldn't tell.

I jumped down and examined my hand. There were no marks, but my palm still tingled from the energy of the ball.

"What is going on?" I exclaimed, my eyes locked on the lion's mouth.

It said nothing.

Rain began to fall. Weird. Only one lonely cloud floated above us.

Kyle grabbed my arm and pulled me back from the lion.

"What's wrong?" I asked.

"Look!" Kyle pointed straight up at the top of the China Gate.

My mouth dropped open. The dragon was now a brilliant shade of jade. The spines on its back jutted up like a row of shark fins. It shook itself like a wet dog, sending water everywhere. The dragon was alive!

CHAPTER TWO

The dragon's giant head swung to the left and the right, its bright green eyes wide with wonder. Then the beautiful creature slithered to the edge of the roof and peered down at us.

Kyle shouted, "Monster!"

The dragon screeched, leapt off the China Gate and floated to the ground as gracefully as a butterfly. Kyle hid behind me. The beast skittered away on its four giant claws. They looked like rooster claws.

I sprinted to my mountain bike and hopped on.

"Hailey! Where are you going?" Kyle shouted.

I had to catch up to the dragon. It snaked around a corner.

"Wait for me!" Kyle cried.

I wheeled around the corner and into an alley. The dragon was gone. All I could see were a dumpster beside a telephone pole and a large puddle. The only place the dragon could be hiding was inside the dumpster. I hopped off my bike and crept toward it.

I inched open the lid. The stench of garbage shot up my nose—a blend of dirty gym socks, rotten bananas and scared skunk. I gagged as I pushed the lid higher. Giant black garbage bags filled the dumpster almost to the top.

There was no room for another bag, let alone a dragon.

Kyle skidded to a stop.

"You saw how beautiful the dragon was, didn't you?" I asked.

"Are you kidding me? Did you see its teeth? It could have snapped us in half and had us for a snack."

"It looked more scared than angry." I brushed my hair from my eyes and searched for any sign of the creature.

"Let's get out of here." Kyle lurched ahead, then stopped and pointed down the alley.

"Hey!" he hollered. "What are you doing?"

Two scruffy teenagers were picking up my bike.

"That's mine!" I shouted.

The long-haired one got on my bike. Kyle and I rushed over.

"Get away from my bike!"

"Don't see your name on it," he sneered.

"Finders keepers," his friend added, spitting on the pavement.

"Give back the bike," Kyle ordered.

The lanky teen grinned at his friend. "You could use a bike, Zak."

"Yeah. And this kid's ride looks sweet." Zak grabbed Kyle's handlebars and shoved Kyle off his bike. His friend laughed as Kyle fell to the ground.

We were alone against the bullies.

"Hey! Don't you dare take our bikes," I roared.

"Who's going to stop us? You?" The tall boy glared at me.

"I'm going to call the police."

Zak climbed onto Kyle's bike. "We'll be long gone by then."

GRRRR!

The teens' mouths dropped open. They pointed behind me. I turned around. The dragon towered over us.

CHAPTER THREE

"What in the world is *that*?" the long-haired boy squeaked.

Zak backed up. "I think I need a new pair of shorts."

The dragon reared up, baring its yellow teeth and slashing the air with its rooster claws. "Leave the bikes!" a female voice boomed.

The bikes clattered to the pavement as the teens fled the scene.

The dragon lowered herself to the ground. She cocked her head to one side and narrowed her eyes as she surveyed the alley.

Kyle grabbed my arm. "Let's get out of here!"

I didn't budge. "I can't believe she can talk."

The dragon leaned closer. I inched back as she breathed on us, bathing us in the scent of jasmine. She flashed a toothy grin.

"Are you going to eat us?" Kyle asked.

The dragon's eyes went wide, and she shook her head. "Eat you? That's disgusting."

"Sorry," he mumbled.

I stepped forward. "My name is Hailey. This is Kyle. Who are you?"

"I am Zhu," she said. "Where am I?"

"Edmonton," I said.

"Where is that?" she asked.

"In Alberta," I said. "Canada?"

She shook her head. "I have not heard of any of these places."

"Where are you from?" Kyle asked.

"The Middle Kingdom."

I scrunched up my face. "The Middle Kingdom? Never heard of it. How did you get here anyway?"

She shook her head. "One moment I was bringing water to the farmers in the fields, and the next I was here. I don't know what happened."

"Are you sure you're not going to eat us?" Kyle asked.

The dragon narrowed her eyes. "Well, human, are you planning to eat me?"

"Of course not," Kyle said. "Why would you think that?"

"The same reason you think I would eat you."

"Don't be scared," I said. "We're not going to hurt you. Can I touch you?"

She nodded. I approached Zhu and stroked her skin. The green scales felt smooth and moist.

"Amazing. Touch her, Kyle. Feels like snakeskin."

He shook his head.

"My grandpa said you shouldn't be afraid of new things," I said.

"I'm pretty sure he wasn't talking about dragons."

"Kyle, she saved us from those bullies," I said.

"Is this a place I should fear?" Zhu asked. "I think I should return home."

"No, you're safe here," I said.

"I need to get back."

"We'll have to figure out a way to get you home. But for now you'll be okay with us."

Zhu spotted the baggie of gummies in Kyle's hand. "What is that?"

"Candy," he said. "They're called Chewy Worms. Want one?"

She opened her mouth, and he tossed a yellow treat into it. Kyle really hated the lemon ones, but Zhu loved it. She sat up like a dog and begged for more. He tossed her another.

"She's going to attract attention," I said. "We'll have to hide her somehow."

"She can squeeze into my backpack."

"Not funny, Kyle."

"Well, I think I could fit," Zhu said.

I raised an eyebrow. "Really? How?"

She smiled. "Watch."

CHAPTER FOUR

Zhu curled into a small ball, and her body became water, pooling at my feet. Two eyes appeared on the surface and blinked at us. "Will this work?"

"Amazing!" I said. "How did you do that?"

The puddle swirled. "It's one of my special powers."

"Cool!"

Kyle fished an empty water bottle out of his backpack. "How do we get her in here?"

Before I could answer, the pool of water jetted up and neatly poured itself into the bottle. Kyle gasped.

Two eyes blinked at us from inside the bottle. A bubble rose to the top and popped.

"Now what do we do?" Kyle asked.

"Do you want to take a tour?" I asked Zhu.

"Yes, but first do you have more of that sweet treat?" she asked.

Kyle nodded. He fished a lemon Chewy Worm out of the baggie and dropped it into the bottle. The water swirled around the gummy as it disappeared bit by bit.

"Wow!" Kyle and I said at the same time.

When the candy was gone, I grabbed the water bottle. We hopped on our bikes. First destination, city hall. A massive glass pyramid towered over the main square. Just in front of the building, kids splashed in a wading pool and danced around a fountain. Across the street a juggler entertained a large crowd. We had arrived in the middle of a summer festival.

The water in the bottle swirled and formed a tiny dragon head. Zhu's jade eyes widened at the kids playing in the fountain. "Wow! Incredible!" she burbled. "So much water that they can afford to splash in it."

"Don't you have water where you come from?"

"Not this much. I am the bringer of water, and I spend most of my days helping farmers get enough to grow their crops."

"Wait. I thought dragons breathed fire," Kyle said.

"Fire? No. I am a water dragon," Zhu said. "I fear fire."

Her head bobbed up and down in the bottle. She reminded me of the jade dragon ornament Grandpa Wong had kept on the living room mantel.

Grandpa Wong used to let me hold the ornament. He'd told me what the dragon means in China. "Hailey, the Chinese dragon is very different from the western one. In North America it is a monster that has bat wings, breathes fire, destroys villages and steals gold. In China the dragon is a symbol of power and strength. It can fly without wings because it can make itself lighter than air, and it brings good luck to everyone."

"I like the Chinese dragon," I said.

"So do I." Grandpa Wong put the ornament back on the mantel. "Shall we play some Go?"

"Yes!"

He nodded and separated the white stones from the black stones on the game board.

"Place your stones on the grid and try to surround one of mine," he explained. "When you capture it, you can take it off the board. The winner is the one who captures the most stones."

"Can't I just grab yours off the board?" I said. "Like this?" I grabbed a black stone.

He laughed. "Yes, but then I could do the same." He scooped up all the white stones with one hand.

"I like our game," I said.

We'd spent the rest of the afternoon seeing who could grab the stones off the board faster. That's what I liked the most about Grandpa Wong. He knew when to play the game by the rules and when to have fun. With him, anything was possible. I could only imagine what he would have thought about a dragon coming to life.

The water in Kyle's bottle gushed up like a tiny water fountain. Zhu's eyes appeared at the top. "What is that sound?" she asked.

Kyle glanced at the food truck parked behind us. "I bet she hears the mini doughnuts in the fryer."

"No, wait," Zhu said coming from farther away."

"Which way?" I asked.

"Beyond the fountain," she said. "Let's go!"

CHAPTER FIVE

Kyle capped the bottle and we took off in search of the sound. We pedaled behind the glass pyramid, wheeled by the museum and headed north. From inside the bottle, Zhu gave us directions. "To the right. Straight. To the left. No, right. Keep going straight now."

We rode past downtown apartments, an empty warehouse and an auto repair shop before old houses started to line the street. We were near my neighborhood.

"I don't hear anything," Kyle said. "Do you still hear it?"

"Yes," Zhu said.

We rode down the block.

"Is it getting louder?" I asked.

"Yes!"

"Okay. What does it sound like?" Kyle asked. "Maybe that can help us find what you're hearing."

"It sounds like distant thunder."

I searched the sky for storm clouds. Not a cloud in the sky. We rode ahead another block.

"Stop!" Zhu said. "Do you hear it?"

Ahead of us was a railroad crossing for the city's passenger trains. There were two sets of tracks. I searched left and right for the source of the sound Zhu could hear. Nothing. Then the warning bell began to ring, and the zebra-striped barricade came down in front of us. The water began to slosh in the bottle.

"It's getting louder," Zhu said.

The bottle vibrated.

"One of my kind is here!"

Kyle scratched his head. "Is she talking about the train?"

The train hurtled past the crossing and into a tunnel. The lid popped off the bottle, and a stream of water shot out. The water grew in size and changed into the jade-green form of a huge dragon.

Zhu danced up and down on her hind legs, then floated after the speeding train.

"Wait!" I cried. "That's not a dragon!"

The train was going too fast for Zhu to catch it. She looked back at us and broke into a wide smile.

"I hear another one coming!" she shouted.

She floated to the mouth of the tunnel and planted herself on the rails in front of it.

Kyle clutched my arm. "We have to get her off the tracks!"

CHAPTER SIX

Dirt and gravel kicked up from our tires as we sped toward Zhu. We had to get to her before the train did. I screeched to a stop beside the tracks and yelled, "Zhu, get out of the way!"

She ignored me and stayed planted in front of the tunnel.

Kyle leaned over his handlebars and screamed, "Get off the tracks!"

She didn't budge.

"Kyle, give me the water bottle!"

He grabbed the bottle and tossed it at me. I held it high in the air. "Zhu, you're not safe there. Get back inside the bottle. Please."

She peeked over her shoulder, sniffed and shook her head before returning her attention to the tunnel.

"You're in danger!" I waved for her to get off the tracks.

"The train's not a dragon," Kyle said. "It's a machine that carries people."

"No, he's like me," Zhu said. "He can show me the way home."

"Zhu!" I shouted. "If you don't get off the tracks, the train's going to crash into you. You're going to get hurt!"

"He will help me," Zhu said. She refused to move. The clack of the steel wheels grew louder. Time was running out.

Kyle clapped his hands. "I have an idea."

"What?"

He reached into his pocket and produced the baggie of Chewy Worms. "Zhu! Look what I have."

She slowly turned around. As soon as she saw the candy, her eyes lit up.

"Want a juicy, delicious gummy?" Kyle cooed.

She licked her lips. The train was getting closer. I could see its lights shining through the tunnel.

"You can have more candy, but only if you come here first," I said.

The clack of the wheels grew louder.

"Or we'll eat them all ourselves," Kyle said.

Zhu took one last look at the tunnel. Then she bounded off the tracks and scampered toward Kyle and me. He dangled the yellow gummy, luring Zhu farther from the tracks. Behind her the train hurtled out of the tunnel and over the spot where she had been waiting moments before.

Zhu turned to follow the train, but I grabbed her leg. "Look in the windows."

She narrowed her gaze. In the passenger cars we saw people glued to their smartphones.

"There are people in his belly," she said. "He ate them? What kind of dragon eats people?"

"No, Zhu. It's a train. It carries people," Kyle said.

"He's not a dragon?" Zhu asked.

I shook my head. "Sorry. It's not."

Her eyes filled with tears. "I miss my home."

As I looked up, there was a rumble of thunder. Clouds began to gather overhead, and a soft rain started to fall.

"Give her another gummy."

Kyle nodded and tossed a red one at Zhu. She caught it and chewed. "Mmm.

Good. Not as tart as the yellow one but still good."

"Let's find you more lemon ones," I offered.

She bounced up and down. Suddenly the rain stopped, and the smell of jasmine filled the air. The scent was so familiar. I had smelled it somewhere else, but I couldn't remember where.

Zhu began to dance and clap her front legs together. "Chewy Worms! Chewy Worms!"

I glanced at the sky. The clouds were gone.

I leaned over and whispered to Kyle, "I think she makes it rain when she's sad."

Kyle searched the skies. "No way. You think she has that power?"

"Well, she said she brings water to the farmers," I said. "How else do you think she does it?"

Kyle shrugged. "I have no clue, but I'd hate to see what happens if she gets really upset."

CHAPTER SEVEN

When I got home, I sneaked Zhu into my bedroom. I didn't want my parents to know a dragon was in our house. Mom would freak out at the mess Zhu might make, and Dad would probably want to sell her on eBay.

I pulled out Kyle's water bottle and poured the water into the fish tank beside my bed. Zhu swirled around in the tank and changed into a guppy-sized version of herself. She chased an angelfish behind the fake treasure chest, then swam to the surface and poked her head out of the water. She rested her front legs on the edge of the tank.

"Can you make yourself any size?" I asked.

She nodded. "Large or small. Whatever size I need to be. As long as I am calm. If I get upset, it's harder to hold myself in another form."

"That's pretty fantastic."

"No, I think what you have here is amazing," she said. "So much water."

She pushed off the tank edge and floated on her back. She spit water up like a fountain, splashing it all over herself.

"Tomorrow I'll show you how I can fill up a sink with water to wash dishes," I joked.

"Water just to clean dishes? Why don't you use sand?" she asked.

"Because that's how much water we have," I said.

"Truly amazing." She spouted more water and let it shower over her.

The next morning I waited until my parents had left for work before bringing Zhu out of my room. She watched as I turned on the tap and let the water run over the dirty dishes from breakfast.

"You can bring the water just like that?" she said, swatting the tap on and off with her claw. "Water on! Water off! Wheeeeee!"

"Would you like some jook?" I asked, trying to get her away from the sink.

She turned off the tap and drummed her claws against each other. "Is it like the sweet treats from yesterday?"

I shook my head. "It's rice porridge. My grandpa loved to eat it in the morning with cut-up pieces of Chinese doughnut. If he couldn't get a Chinese doughnut, he'd just throw in fish crackers. It's tasty."

I spooned some jook into a small bowl and set it on the table in front of Zhu. She sniffed the bowl a couple of times, then peered at me with big eyes. "No Chewy Worms?"

"No. Sorry. Kyle has them."

"When is he getting here?" she asked.

"Try the jook," I said. "You'll like it."

She sniffed the bowl again and pushed it away. "It smells funny."

"Grandpa Wong always said, 'Don't be afraid of something new. This might be the start of your next great adventure.'"

"I think I've had enough adventure for now," Zhu said.

"If you try it, I might be able to find some Chewy Worms. The lemon ones."

Zhu wrapped both her front claws around the bowl and licked the white porridge. She looked up, her eyes wide with delight. Rice porridge dripped from her lips. I covered my mouth to keep from laughing.

"See? Not so bad," I said.

"I like it." She lifted the bowl to her mouth and slurped it all back. Then she slammed the bowl on the table with a messy grin. "Can I have some more?"

I filled her bowl again.

Several bowls of jook later, Zhu was finally full. I washed the dishes while she sat on the counter and swatted the tap to turn the water off and on. The water splashed all over me, and she laughed.

"So much water to play with," she said. More water flew my way.

"Well, let's not use all of it," I said, mopping my face.

Suddenly she stood up and bonked her head on a cabinet. "I smell Chewy Worms!"

"Where?"

"Outside!" She hopped down and floated toward the front door.

"Wait!" I called, chasing after her.

In the front yard Kyle had leaned against a tree with the baggie of gummies. He was watching some kids play road hockey. Before I could stop her, Zhu rushed outside. The kids dropped their hockey sticks and gawked at the giant creature now sitting on her hind legs and panting like a puppy.

No one said a thing. Zhu lowered her head and whimpered. Kyle fished a yellow gummy out of the baggie and dangled it over her mouth. She snatched the candy between her teeth and scampered toward the house.

The kids rushed over, clamoring with questions.

"What is that thing?"

"Where did it come from?"

"Can we pet it?"

"What's with the bag of candy?"

I held up my hands to calm everyone down. "She won't hurt anyone. She's a Chinese dragon. She loves Chewy Worms."

Zhu lowered her head so the kids could stroke her scaly mane. Everyone crowded around for a turn to touch her.

Though they had never seen a dragon before, the kids were more curious than afraid. Zhu loved the attention, and she rolled on her back for tummy rubs from a boy wearing an Arizona Coyotes hockey jersey.

Suddenly there was a screech from across the street. It was Mrs. Evans, a part-time fitness trainer and full-time snoop. "What are you kids up to?!"

Mrs. Evans was the kind of person who loved to yell at kids and call the cops on troublemakers. I froze at the thought of what Mrs. Evans would do if she saw a dragon on her street.

We had to hide Zhu *now*.

CHAPTER EIGHT

I pushed through the crowd of kids and whispered, "Zhu, change."

She arched an eyebrow.

"No time to explain," I said. "Change. Into anything! Just do it fast."

She cranked her head around so that she was nose to shirt with the boy giving her tummy rubs. She eyed the coyote mascot on his jersey and puffed her cheeks. Her entire body sprouted fur, and her claws turned into paws. She was becoming a coyote.

All the kids jumped back, shocked by her transformation.

Mrs. Evans spotted coyote Zhu and shrieked, "Everyone! Get away! It's a coyote! It might have rabies. Move back!"

Storm clouds began to gather over my house. Zhu slunk behind me and whimpered.

Mrs. Evans grabbed Kyle's arm. "Get away from that beast immediately. It's dangerous!"

Kyle yelped. "Ow! Let go."

Zhu lunged at Mrs. Evans and let out a loud yip.

"It's attacking!" Mrs. Evans screeched, using Kyle as a shield.

I pulled Zhu away.

Thunder cracked. The clouds opened up and rain poured down. The wet kids sped off to their dry homes.

"Run!" Mrs. Events cried. "It will eat you alive! I've seen it on YouTube."

Kyle backed away. "No she won't. She's not dangerous."

Zhu growled at Mrs. Evans, who took off.

Then Zhu's coyote tail began to turn back into a dragon tail.

"You'll be safer inside," I said, steering Zhu toward my house. But I didn't need to worry, as Mrs. Evans was hurtling at breakneck speed back to her house.

The rain was falling even harder. Kyle helped me push Zhu into the house. Once inside, she began to shed fur all over the floor, and she changed back into a dragon.

Hail began to pelt on the roof. Zhu ran behind the couch in the living room. I hoped she would be able to calm down now so the rain would stop.

"Why was that lady so angry?" Zhu asked.

"You did nothing wrong," Kyle said, as he shook the water off his hair. "Mrs. Evans is always like that."

I grabbed a towel from the hall closet so Kyle could dry off. I checked the window for nosy neighbors. No one. I drew the curtains closed.

"It's okay, Zhu," I said. "You can come out. No one's going to hurt you."

I headed to my bedroom to change and find a T-shirt in my drawer that might fit Kyle.

When I got back Zhu was curled up on the shag carpet, and Kyle was stroking the back of her head. He had come a long way since the day before, when he was terrified of Zhu. The rain had let up, and the fragrance of jasmine hung in the air. I wished I could remember where else I had smelled that aroma.

I tossed Kyle my shirt. "This should fit," I said.

He scrunched up his face. "You want me to wear your shirt?"

"You want to be wet all day?"

"I'll stick with my shirt," he said as he slipped into the bathroom to dry off his clothes.

Zhu lifted her head. "Sorry I caused all this trouble."

"No, you did nothing wrong," I said. "Some people just don't understand."

"I have to return home," she said. "I can't stay here any longer. The farmers need me."

"Kyle and I will help you," I said.

Outside a car door slammed. I walked to the window and cracked the curtains open to take a peek. My stomach twisted into a knot. A white van had parked out front.

It had writing on the side. It said *Animal Control.*

CHAPTER NINE

"Mrs. Evans must have called them," Kyle said, peeking out the window at the Animal Control officers who'd jumped out of the van.

The uniformed woman put on heavy black gloves while her partner pulled out a long pole with a loop of wire on one end.

"They think she's a coyote," Kyle said. "They want to capture her."

Zhu inched toward the couch. "Are they going to hurt me?"

A crack of thunder shook the house. I reached out and stroked Zhu's scaly head. "We're not going to let anyone hurt you. It's going to be okay, Zhu. Shh."

Knock, knock, knock.

We froze.

A woman's voice boomed. "Open up. Animal Control."

"We can't let them in," I hissed.

"Hailey, Mrs. Evans saw us take Zhu into the house."

"I'm not welcome here," Zhu said. "I need to get home."

"What if she turns herself into water and we hide her in the sink?" Kyle suggested.

"Can you do that?" I asked Zhu.

"Maybe. I'm not sure," she said. "I'd have to concentrate, but I'm scared."

"Kyle, plug the drain in the sink."

Zhu and I followed Kyle to the kitchen while we talked. "Please. Just try. You'll be safe that way."

She nodded, then closed her eyes and puffed her cheeks. But nothing happened. She puffed her cheeks again and twisted her body to one side. Still nothing.

"Take a breath and try again," I said.

She did, but she still couldn't transform into water.

Zhu shook her head. "I'm too upset. I can't focus."

More knocking. This time louder. "We have reports that there's a coyote in your house. Answer the door."

"They're not going to go away," Kyle said.

There was a clap of thunder. Zhu was still terrified.

"Out the back," I whispered, and I pushed Zhu toward the kitchen.

We stopped at the back door. I spotted the officer with the pole in the alley.

"Ack! There's no escape!" Kyle cried. "We're surrounded."

Suddenly I had an idea.

I turned to Zhu. "Can you fly us out of here?"

"I think so," she said.

I opened the door. She crawled out and lowered her body so we could climb onto her back. Her scales were slick and smooth. I tried to find a spot to hold and settled for hugging her body. Kyle got on behind me.

"Ready," I said.

Whoosh! The air rushed past my face. I held on tight as my stomach did flip-flops. When I looked back, Kyle's grin was wide enough to light up the sky.

"Yeehaw!" he shouted.

Below us, my house looked as small as a doll's house. Neither of the Animal Control officers had spotted us. The one in the alley was using his pole to lift the lids of garbage cans, while the one in front kept pounding on the door.

Kyle whooped like a cowboy. "Yahooo! We're flying! I can't believe we're flying!"

Zhu peeked back at us. "Where should I go?"

I had no idea.

CHAPTER TEN

We soared over the city. Kyle whooped and cheered as we approached downtown. The storm clouds began to lighten.

"You still haven't told me where you want me to go," Zhu said.

I had no answer. I chewed on my lower lip, trying to think of how we could get her home. Grandpa Wong would have known what to do. I wished he was here now. I missed our talks at dim sum and our visits to the Chinese lions.

The statues! The answer was suddenly as bright as the sun that broke through the clouds.

"Zhu! I know where to go!"

She craned her head to look back. "Where?"

"Fly back to where we found you. The China Gate!"

"Why do you want to go there?" Kyle shouted.

"Do you remember the lion statues? I think they're the reason Zhu is here."

"What do you mean?" Zhu asked.

"I wished for it. I was missing my grandpa, and I thought about how much the dragons had meant to him. I hated that the city is going to take down the gate."

"What did you wish for?" Kyle asked.

"That Zhu didn't have to get taken down. I wished there was a way to save her. The next thing I knew, she was alive."

Zhu's eyes widened. "Do you think wishing on the stone lions can send me home?"

I nodded. "I can't be totally sure, but we have to try."

Zhu sped up.

Kyle laughed. "If I had known the wishes would actually come true, I'd have wished for more than Chewy Worms."

"No you wouldn't."

He laughed. "Maybe. Maybe not."

I spotted the dim sum restaurant. I wondered what Grandpa Wong would have made of the dragon. Maybe he would have said to enjoy the new adventure. I missed him so much.

As we got closer, I saw the English letters and the Chinese characters running up and down the neon sign.

"We are here!" I cried. "The China Gate is around the next corner."

Zhu dipped lower and circled over the street. There were a few people, but they were more interested in their phones than in us.

We landed in a parking lot across the street from the restaurant. Kyle and I hopped off. The lot was empty. So far, so good.

"Quick, Zhu," I said. "Turn into water. We don't want to attract any attention. We're going to get you home."

"Home!" She beamed as she melted into a puddle of water.

"Okay, Kyle," I said. "Hand me the water bottle."

He shook his head. "Sorry. I thought you grabbed it."

"Seriously?" I said. "We can't move her around without a bottle or a container."

"I have an idea," Zhu burbled.

A furry head rose out of the puddle as Zhu transformed into a coyote.

"I think that should work," I said. "But we'll have to be careful."

"Let's find the lions," she yipped.

"They're at the China Gate," I said as I walked toward the corner.

The screech of a saw cutting through concrete filled the air. Orange barricades blocked off the street.

"Stay here," I told Kyle and Zhu.

I jogged ahead to get a view of the China Gate. The red pillars that held up the golden archway were bare. The pagoda roof rested on a flatbed trailer. Workers were gathered around the base of each pillar. My heart dropped.

The stone lions were gone.

CHAPTER ELEVEN

Jackhammers pounded the sidewalk, breaking the cement into rubble. The city workers had already taken down most of the China Gate. I headed to the barricade for a closer view, but a worker wearing an orange vest waved me away.

"You'll have to take a detour," she said. "This street's closed for the day."

"What happened to the stone lions?"

"The lions? Oh, they've already taken them to storage."

"Where is that?" I asked.

She ignored my question and jogged into the street to direct traffic away from the construction.

Our only way of sending Zhu home was gone. I ran back to tell my friends. "The workers already took the lions, but we can follow the flatbed trailer when they take the arch away. They're probably going to move the gate to the same place they took the lions."

Kyle looked over his shoulder. "Yeah, but I think we have another problem."

"What?"

He pointed across the street. Several people were staring at us. Well, to be more accurate, they were staring at Zhu the coyote.

A man in a suit yelled, "Get away! That's a wild animal."

"It's okay!" I yelled back, but the man ran toward us.

"We have to go," Kyle said.

We sprinted away. Zhu took the lead, running past a group of office workers. They yelled and jumped out of the way. A few started to make calls on their phones. One of them snapped a picture.

"Oh, no! I think they're calling Animal Control," Kyle huffed.

Zhu asked, "What will they do if they find me?"

"They're not going to catch you," I said, glancing at the clouds darkening overhead.

Kyle grabbed my arm. "Do we need the China Gate stone lions, or will any stone lion work?"

"Good question. But where can we find another stone lion?"

He shrugged. "I have no clue, but I bet we could find out there." He pointed down the street at the library.

I beamed. "Yes! You're amazing!"

He tapped his head. "Not just a place to hang baseball caps."

We raced to the library. I had no idea how to find the information we needed, but I was pretty sure a librarian could help. The only problem was, we couldn't go into the library with a coyote.

"Zhu's going to have to wait out here," I said.

"But people are going to spot her."

I put my hand on Zhu's head. "Can you turn into a puddle and wait for us here?"

She closed her eyes, and the fur fell off her body. Water pooled around her paws, and she melted into the puddle, leaving just two eyes blinking up at us. "Hurry back," she burbled.

"We will!" I grabbed Kyle and pulled him toward the library's main doors. Inside we found a librarian wearing a black T-shirt with *Information Ninja* on the front.

"Hi, can you help us?" I asked. "We're trying to find Chinese lions in Edmonton."

The young man smiled at me. "Sure, let's see what we can find." He led us to a computer terminal. His fingers danced across the keyboard as he entered text into the computer. In a flash, the screen showed an image of the lions at the China Gate.

Kyle leaned forward. "Yes, we saw those ones. Are there others?"

"Hmm. Well, I remember a magazine article from a few months ago. Let me see if I can locate it," he said. "Follow me."

He headed up the steps to the second floor. Newspapers hung from wooden racks, and magazines filled the shelves along the back wall. The librarian ran his finger along the magazines until he found the right one. He grabbed it and flipped through the pages.

"Ah, yes. I was right. The Chinese Garden has stone lions."

Kyle raised an eyebrow and scratched his head. "Where is that?"

"In the river valley. It's about three blocks from here. I'll give you directions."

I grinned. "Thanks."

The librarian scribbled down the directions on a slip of paper. I thanked him again, and we started to head out of the building. At the doorway I grabbed Kyle's arm. The Animal Control van was rolling down the street. They were looking for Zhu.

CHAPTER TWELVE

Storm clouds swirled over the library. The tip of Zhu's snout began to rise out of the water as she returned to her dragon form. I knelt down beside the swirling puddle. "Shh, shh, Zhu. Don't be scared."

A flash of lightning told me she wasn't calming down.

"Hailey, we need to get to the Chinese Garden," Kyle said. "Hey, maybe it's good that she's upset."

"Why?"

He pointed at the clouds. "People will want to get out of the rain."

I clapped my hand on his back. "Great idea! Zhu, can you make it rain?"

Her head was sticking out of the puddle. "Yes. How hard?"

"Make it a downpour," I said.

We heard a huge crack of thunder and then the clouds opened up. A river of rain poured down, and people scattered for shelter. No one was looking our way. Zhu's head rose out of the puddle as the rest of the water changed into her dragon body. We hopped on her back, and she flew straight up.

"Which way?" I yelled at Kyle.

"To the left and past the convention center!"

Zhu soared high above the traffic. Just past the convention center a flight of wooden stairs led down to the river valley. We landed at the top of the stairs. In the field below we could see a gazebo with a pagoda roof, and a stone bridge over a pond. On the other side of the pond, two stone lions were perched. These gray lions weren't as magnificent as the ones from the China Gate. They were about half the size, but they were just what we needed.

"Let's go!" I said.

The thunder boomed as we raced down the stairs.

"Almost home, Zhu," I said. "Keep going!"

"Hailey! Hold on! There's someone down there!"

I froze. A jogger had taken shelter in the gazebo. I grabbed Zhu by the claw. "Quick. Change yourself."

She closed her eyes and puffed her cheeks. The claw in my hand turned into a furry paw. She was a coyote again.

"No, change to water," I said.

Too late. There was a shout below. The jogger had spotted us.

"Get away from that coyote!" she screamed as she yanked out her smartphone and began to make a call.

"We have to get to the Chinese lions before Animal Control shows up!" Kyle yelled.

"Down the stairs!"

Zhu bounded down the steps with the two of us right behind her. We had to move fast.

The jogger shouted into her phone, "The coyote is going to attack the kids. Hurry!"

"Think of the Chinese lion, Zhu!" I said, trying to calm her. "You're going to go home."

"Home," she said. "Yes."

We reached the base of the stairs. The jogger waved her arms and charged at Zhu. "Scat. Get away. Vamoose!"

Zhu arched her back and growled. I could see her dragon scales peeking through the fur on her back.

The jogger slipped on the wet grass and scrambled back to her feet. She ran toward the stairs, screaming.

"She's going to get help," I said. "We have to do this now!"

"How much time do you need?" Kyle asked.

"I have no idea. I don't know how long it took to wish Zhu here in the first place. I'm not even sure it will work."

"Please send me home," Zhu begged. Rain poured down, washing away her fur and exposing her jade-green scales. She had returned to her dragon form. There was no hiding her now.

Kyle grabbed my arm. "I'll buy you more time."

"How?"

"I'm going to make sure no one bothers you while you make your wish." He sped toward the stairs. The jogger was already halfway to the top.

"Come on!" I led Zhu to the stone bridge.

"This looks like my home, but not quite."

"You'll see your home soon enough," I said, crossing the bridge and heading toward the stone lions on the other side.

I could hear Kyle's voice. "I know where the coyote is!"

I grabbed Zhu's claw and drew her to the side of the bridge. I peered through the stone pillars and saw Kyle halfway up the stairs. He was waving at two Animal Control officers.

"This way!" Kyle yelled.

He ran down the stairs with the two officers on his heels. I pulled Zhu close and put a finger to my lips. "Shhh."

CHAPTER THIRTEEN

I held Zhu close as I watched Kyle head toward the river. The officers were right behind him. They didn't spot us.

Kyle led them past the park and down the hill. I waited until they were out of sight, then motioned Zhu to follow me. We headed down the stone path toward the lions. I hoped the wish was going to work. But what if it didn't? No. I couldn't worry about it. This *had* to work.

We reached the lion nearest us—the one with the open mouth. I turned to Zhu. "This is your way home. I just have to make a wish on the stone ball in the lion's mouth."

She nodded. "You are a good friend. I am in your debt."

A lump formed in my throat. I couldn't say a thing, but I leaned in and hugged Zhu. The scent of jasmine filled my nose. I knew then what the scent reminded me of. Tea! Jasmine tea had been Grandpa Wong's favorite drink.

"It's time," I said, pulling away.

I reached into the lion's mouth and touched the stone ball.

"I wish Zhu—" I stopped. I knew I had to send Zhu back home, but I didn't want to lose her. Someone else I cared about was going to leave me. For a second I thought about making a different wish.

"Are you all right?" Zhu asked.

"I'm fine," I lied. I didn't want her to go. I wanted her to stay, just like I'd wanted Grandpa Wong to stay.

"Hailey?"

I rolled my hand over the stone ball in the lion's mouth. "I wish…I wish…"

I stopped as I remembered the last thing Grandpa Wong had said to me in the hospital. "Hailey, don't be afraid. I'll always be here in your memories."

My eyes teared up. I missed Grandpa Wong so much. And I would miss Zhu as well. But I knew he was right.

I rubbed the stone ball. "I wish Zhu could go home."

The clouds began to break apart, and a rainbow appeared in front of us.

Zhu broke into a huge grin. "The way home!"

I removed my hand from the lion's mouth.

"I will miss you and Kyle."

"I hope you'll come back to visit our world, Zhu."

The aroma of jasmine tea wafted up into my nose.

"Or you could come to the Middle Kingdom. What was it your grandfather said? 'A new thing might be the start of your next adventure.'"

I beamed. "Goodbye, Zhu."

"Until we meet again."

She flew up, her jade body curling around the rainbow like a streamer. I watched her rise into the sky and disappear. All that was left was the rainbow.

"Hailey!" Kyle shouted.

I looked across the park.

Kyle was headed toward me. I waved him over.

"Did it work?" he asked.

I gave him a high five. "Zhu's back home."

"Great!"

"Wait, what about the Animal Control officers?" I asked.

"They'll be searching the river valley for hours for that coyote."

I laughed. "Want to make a wish?"

"Well, I could use some more Chewy Worms."

ACKNOWLEDGMENTS

No author walks alone. I'm happy to have so many companions along the journey to help me take this from an idea to a fully formed book. Thank you to Wei Wong, Michelle Chan, Diane Tucker, Debbie Rogosin and the TD Summer Reading Club for being my guides.

MARTY CHAN is an award-winning author of dozens of books for kids, including *Kung Fu Master*, *Haunted Hospital*, *Willpower* and *Kylie the Magnificent* in the Orca Currents line and the award-winning Marty Chan Mystery series. He tours schools and libraries across Canada, using storytelling, stage magic and improv to ignite a passion for reading in kids. He lives in Edmonton.

GRACE CHEN is a Chinese Canadian artist and illustrator. A graduate of Sheridan College's illustration program, Grace has a strong foundation in traditional mediums that greatly influences her current art. She is inspired by moments in her life, the world at large and the works of those around her. Grace lives in Toronto.